AT THE OLD HAUNTED HOUSE

By Helen Ketteman
Illustrated by Nate Wragg

two lions

two lions

For Mary Ann, with love
—H. K.

For my wife, Crystal, and my daughter,
Willow, your love and support makes
every day better than the last.
—N. W.

Published by Two Lions, New York   www.apub.com
Amazon, the Amazon logo, and Two Lions are trademarks of Amazon.com, Inc., or its affiliates.
ISBN-13: 9781477847695   ISBN-10: 1477847693
The illustrations are mixed media, created by combining digital painting and scanned textures.
Book design by Jen Browning. Printed in China. First edition.

At the old haunted house
in a room with no sun
lived a warty green witch
and her wee witchy one.

"SPELL!"
cried the witch.

"POOF!"

cried the one.

And they both practiced spells in the room with no sun.

At the old haunted house
where a cold draft blew
lived a big ma monster
and her wee monsters two.

"STIR!"
called the ma.

"WE STIR!"
cried the two.

And they whirred
and they stirred
while the cold draft blew.

By the old haunted house
in the dead, hollow tree
lived a scrawny black cat
and her wee kittens three.

"SCRATCH!"

cried the mother.

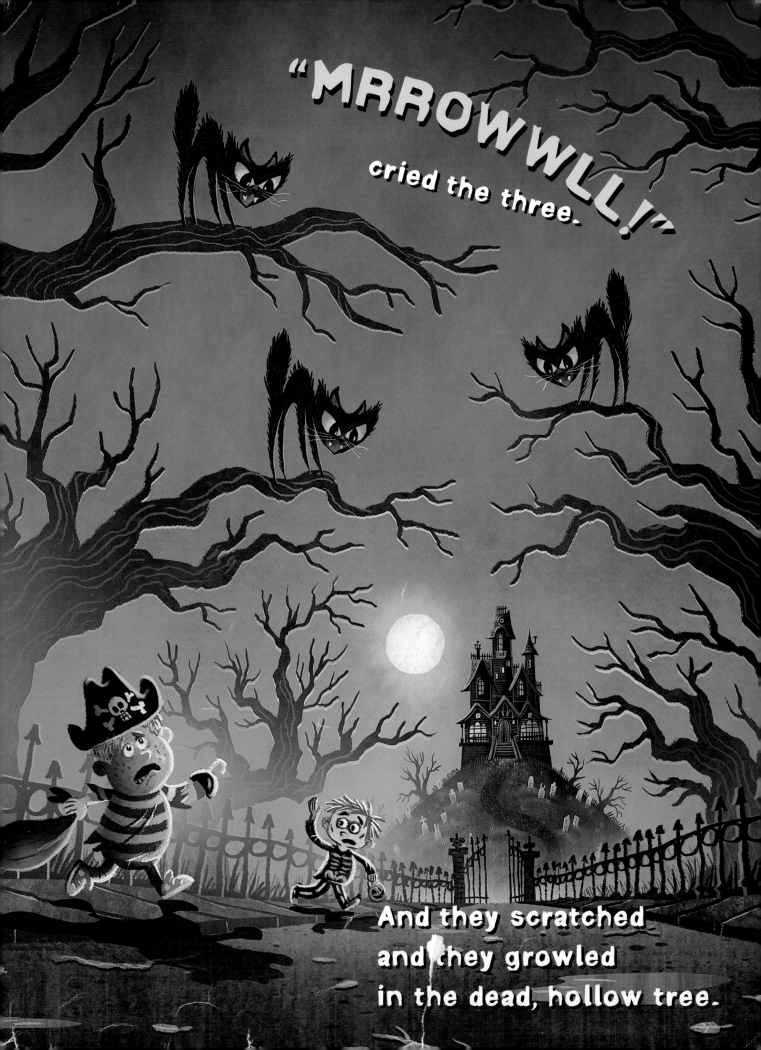

At the old haunted house
with the squeaky old floor
lived a green pa goblin
and his wee goblins four.

At the old haunted house
where scary things jive
lived a ma werewolf
and her wee wolfies five.

"Howl!!"
cried the ma.

"Arrooo

In the old haunted house
in a vault made of bricks
lived a papa vampire
and his little vamps six.

"Show fangs!"
Papa cried.

"Hisssssss!"

went the six.

And they snarled
and they shrieked
in the vault made of bricks.

At the old haunted house,
teaching a lesson,
was a hairy mom bat
and her bitty bats seven.

"Dip-dive!"
cried the mom.

"**Flip-flap!**" went the seven.

...heir **dip-diving lesson.**

By the old haunted house
near the graveyard gate
lived a spooky dad ghost
and his wee ghosties eight.

"Haunt!"
cried the dad.

"Booooo!"

cried the eight.

And they booed
and they floated
through the graveyard gate.

At the old haunted house
half covered with vines
lived a mummy mommy
and her wee mummies nine.

"Mix!"

called the mommy.

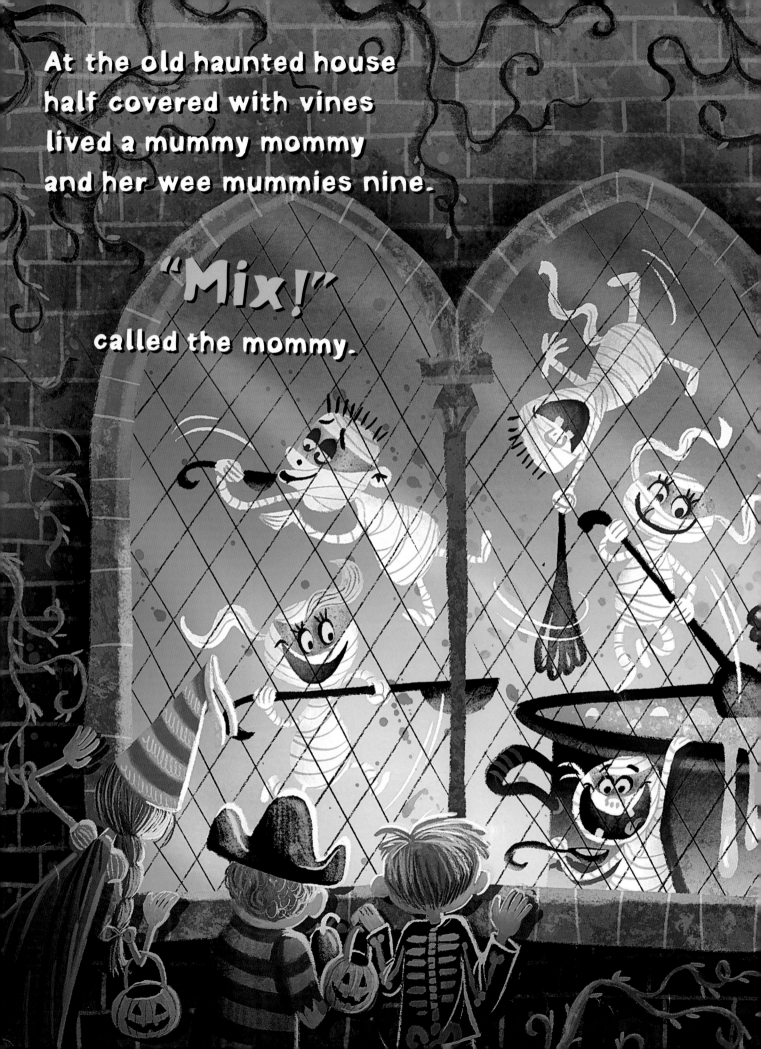

"We mix!"
called the nine.

And they stirred and they mixed
in the house with the vines.

At the old haunted house
in the dusty old den
lived a fat ma spider
and her wee spiders ten.

"Spin!"
called the ma.

"Weave, ho!" said the ten.

And they spun sticky webs
in the dusty old den.

At the old haunted house
the front door C-R-E-A-K-E-D.

"Come in!"
called Ma Mummy.

The monsters made stew!
The mummies made cake!
The witches zapped brew!

The creatures all grinned
as they struck up the band,

and the spiders all swung
on sticky web strands.

The ghosties floated as the music played.